Jetpack Jelly

'Jetpack Jelly'
An original concept by Alice Hemming
© Alice Hemming

Illustrated by Emma Randall

Published by MAVERICK ARTS PUBLISHING LTD
Studio 3A, City Business Centre, 6 Brighton Road,
Horsham, West Sussex, RH13 5BB
© Maverick Arts Publishing Limited January 2019
+44 (0)1403 256941

A CIP catalogue record for this book is available at the British Library.

ISBN 978-1-84886-399-6

Maverick
publishing
www.maverickbooks.co.uk

White

This book is rated as: White Band (Guided Reading)

Jetpack Jelly

By **Alice Hemming**

Illustrated by **Emma Randall**

Chapter 1

The Space Place café was full of jelly. There was red and orange jelly on the counters, purple jelly on the shelves and stripy jelly on the tables.

Zip, Zap and Moondoodle turned up for their usual Friday treat.

"Welcome to my wibbly, wobbly world," said Stacey.

5

"Wow, why is there so much jelly?" asked
Moondoodle.

"Everyone seems to like it," said Stacey.
"Would you like to try some?"

Zip swallowed a spoonful. "Mmm, jellicious!" he
said.

"It's the best jelly ever," agreed Zap.

Stacey smiled. "The only problem is, everyone
wants some. People have ordered jelly for
weddings, jelly for parties, even jelly for
breakfast. I have to deliver all of this by the end
of the day or I'll be working at the weekend."

"But we're supposed to be going to Picnic Planet this weekend," said Zap, miserably.

"I'm trying my best," said Stacey. "Timble has been helping. He made me a hoverboard on Wednesday but I couldn't balance on it with all the jelly. He fitted rocket boosters to my roller boots yesterday but they were no good on the stairs. He says he's got something even better to show me today."

The door opened. Timble staggered in with a large brown box. He grinned and put it on the floor. "This is the answer to your wobbly problem."

Stacey opened the box. "A jetpack! Er, Timble, I've never used one of these before."

"It's quite simple," said Timble. "Put your arms through like this, buckle it here, and press the green button. You shouldn't have any problems – it's like a mini-rocket."

"What's this red button for?" asked Stacey.

"Don't worry about the red button. Only press it in an absolute emergency."

"Ooh, what would happen?"

"Just don't worry about the red button. You won't have to use it," Timble said.

"Ok," said Stacey. "Would you mind watching the café for me, Moondoodle? Then I can make a start on these deliveries."

"Of course," said Moondoodle. "I'll box up all this jelly."

Stacey jetted out of the door with a delivery bag full of plastic boxes.

"This jetpack is going to make my deliveries easy," said Stacey.

Chapter 2

Stacey arrived at her first stop: a tall tower block stretching towards the stars. The sign on the door said Helix Heights.

"This is the one!" said Stacey. "I could take the boring old lift but I know a quicker way."

Stacey pressed the green button. WHOOSH!

She whizzed up the outside of the building.

"That was quick," she said, as she reached the top floor.

She knocked and called, "Jetpack Jelly from the Space Place!"

An excited face appeared from behind a curtain and the window opened.

"Wonderful – my grandchildren will be thrilled," said the lady, taking her box of jelly.

"No problem," called Stacey as the lady closed the window.

"This is so easy! I will deliver all these by lunchtime. I will be ready for Picnic Planet tomorrow."

Stacey patted herself on the back and danced a mid-air jig. She punched the sky with both fists, somersaulted forwards and flipped backward. She began flying back down to the ground. But halfway down she heard an unexpected...

TWANG!

Stacey stopped. The jetpack was still whirring but she was stuck in mid-air. She saw her problem – three pairs of spotty pants, five odd socks and a well-worn T-shirt. Stacey was caught on a washing line.

She pressed the green button but the line was wedged under her jetpack. She tried another somersault but got even more tangled.

"This is bad," she said to herself.

Stacey looked down. The ground was a long way off, so there was no way she could remove the jetpack and drop down.

Music blared out of the building.

Stacey twisted around and peered through the window. Someone was dancing. He was shaking maracas and moving to the beat.

"Help!" she cried. "I'm stuck!"

The figure carried on dancing, his pink sequined jacket flashing.

"Help!" called Stacey, louder this time, and banged on the glass.

The figure turned round. Stacey recognised him at once, despite the rose between his teeth.

Chapter 3

"Astro Pete!" said Stacey.

Astro Pete dropped the flower and looked embarrassed. His red face clashed with his pink jacket. He came and opened the window.

"Spacey Stacey! You've rather caught me by surprise. I was just doing some housework," he mumbled. "I was trying to decide where to put these maracas..."

"I don't care about the dancing," said Stacey. "I'm a bit stuck here. Please help get me down! I promise never to tell anyone about your dancing, ok?"

"Ok," said Pete. He climbed onto the windowsill.

"Take my hand," he said, stretching towards her.

But Pete's shiny trousers were not made for crawling along windowsills. Just as Stacey grabbed his hand, Pete slipped.

"Aaargh!" called Pete, grabbing at the air. Fortunately, he landed with both feet

on a pipe below.

Stacey bent forwards, keeping hold of Pete's hand.

"What are we going to do now?" she asked.

"Use the jetpack?" asked Pete.

Stacey shook her head. "I keep pressing the green button but it doesn't work – look."

"What about the red button?" called Pete.

"Timble said only to use the red button in an absolute emergency."

Pete rolled his eyes.

"This *is* an absolute emergency! Press the red button!"

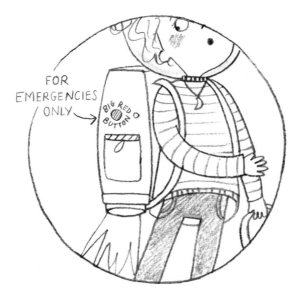

Chapter 4

Spacey Stacey took a deep breath and pressed the red button.

Nothing happened. Pete and Stacey looked at each other nervously.

The jetpack began to make a deep noise.

The deep noise became a rumble. And then...
bang, BANG, BANG!

Stacey jolted forwards, pulling the washing line from the wall. Pete grabbed her around the waist and the jetpack shot off.

They rocketed into the air, past the roof of Helix Heights and towards the bright stars above them.

"Aaaaaaargh!'" called Astro Pete.

Stacey tried moving left and then right but it didn't work. "I can't control it! If we keep heading this way, we'll crash on Planet Stink!"

But then the jetpack made a new noise... bump, bump, bump! POOOF!

A hatch opened
and a giant colourful
cloth billowed out.

"A parachute!" laughed Stacey.
"Timble thinks of everything. We can use
it to glide back!"

The journey back was much smoother than the
journey there. Stacey steered them along.

From up in the clouds they could see buildings
and the tops of trees. The washing line
fluttered out like a tail. Socks and pants flapped
behind them.

"I liked your dancing," said Stacey. "I know you
don't want me to talk about it but I thought you
were brilliant."

"My mum taught me when I was little," said
Pete. "I used to win competitions before I got
into space racing."

"You shouldn't hide it. It is something to be proud of," said Stacey. Pete had stopped listening and was looking past the buildings to the streets below.

"Oh no," said Pete, "I can see a whole crowd of people. Even Jack Boom and Jill Zoom."

"Is that Timble and Moondoodle? And Zip and Zap?" cried Stacey, "Here, hold this jelly and I'll give them a wave."

But Pete was trying to take off his sparkly jacket. He dropped the bag of jelly boxes, which plummeted below them. The lids fell away.

Red, orange and purple jellies tumbled down, like burst balloons.

"I can't watch!" said Stacey, closing her eyes.

"We will cover them all in jelly!" moaned Astro Pete.

But the crowd below didn't look cross. Stacey could hear laughing. People staggered backwards with their mouths open.

One man turned his umbrella upside down to catch as much as he could.

Spacey Stacey and Astro Pete landed safely on the ground to happy cheers.

Chapter 5

Later, back at the Space Place, Stacey was once again boxing up jelly in the kitchen.

"Thanks for making all this extra jelly, Moondoodle."

"It was nothing," said Moondoodle. "It was a quiet afternoon in here."

"There's plenty for this afternoon. I'll need more for next week, though. I've had loads of orders since we dropped the jelly. Everyone thought it was a publicity stunt," said Stacey.

"We thought so too, when we saw Astro Pete in his snazzy costume," said Timble. "If it wasn't planned then why on earth was he dressed like that?"

Stacey pretended not to hear.
She had promised to keep quiet.

"It has all worked out perfectly.
Best of all, there's still time to
go to Picnic Planet this weekend.
Which jelly shall we take with us? Zip
and Zap, you can choose."

Zip and Zap held hands and spun
around in a circle.

"Let's have a bit of everything!
Hooray for Picnic Planet! And
hooray for jetpack jelly!"

The End

Book Bands for Guided Reading

Pink

Red

Yellow

Blue

Green

Orange

Turquoise

Purple

Gold

White

The Institute of Education book banding system is a scale of colours that reflects the various levels of reading difficulty. The bands are assigned by taking into account the content, the language style, the layout and phonics. Word, phrase and sentence level work is also taken into consideration.

Maverick Early Readers are a bright, attractive range of books covering the pink to white bands. All of these books have been book banded for guided reading to the industry standard and edited by a leading educational consultant.

To view the whole Maverick Readers scheme, visit our website at
www.maverickearlyreaders.com

Or scan the QR code above to view our scheme instantly!